HRAFKEL'S SAGA

An Icelandic Story
adapted and retold by
BARBARA SCHILLER
Wood Engravings by Carol Iselin

The Seabury Press
New York

101674

for Thomas,
seven years after the first

❧ ☙

TEXT COPYRIGHT © 1972 BY BARBARA SCHILLER
ILLUSTRATIONS COPYRIGHT © 1972 BY THE SEABURY PRESS
LIBRARY OF CONGRESS CATALOG CARD NUMBER: 72–75703
ISBN: 0–8164–3082–9

DESIGNED BY JUDITH LERNER
PRINTED IN THE UNITED STATES OF AMERICA

SOURCES

THE CHIEF SOURCES for the text are to be found in *Hrafkel's Saga and Other Stories* translated by Hermann Palsson and *Eirik the Red and Other Icelandic Sagas* translated by Gwyn Jones.

Such books as Halldor Hermannsson's *Old Icelandic Literature, The Origins of Icelandic Literature* by G. Turville-Petre, *The Icelandic Saga* by Peter Hallberg and W. P. Ker's *Epic and Romance* were consulted for the literary background.

The Vikings by Holgar Arbman, *The North Atlantic Saga* by Gwyn Jones, *The Vikings* by Johannes Brondsted and *The Vikings* by Frank R. Donovan were interesting and informative for both author and artist.

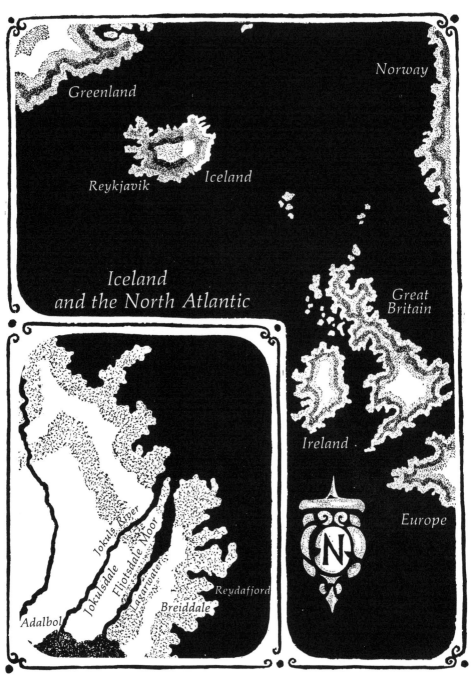

Greenland

Norway

Reykjavik   Iceland

Iceland
and the North Atlantic

Great
Britain

Ireland

Europe

Jokuls River

Jokulsdale

Fljotsdale Moor

Lagarwater

Reydafjord

Adalbol

Breiddale

INSET MAP: *The Eastfjords of Iceland*
where the action of the Saga takes place

INTRODUCTION

ICELAND WAS the last land in which the far-ranging Norsemen of the Viking era made a permanent settlement. The craggy island was then, as it is now, a crumpled land of volcanoes, snowfields, and glaciers—gray and grim in the winter, but gay and surprisingly green during the never-ending days of summer.

The first settlers belong as much to legend as to history, but by 874, Ingolf, a Norwegian, had established himself and his followers in Reykjavik, Iceland's present capital. Within sixty years the country was fully settled. Twenty thousand people lived around the edge of the sea, along the deep fjords, and in the long valleys. Wherever there was pasturage, fresh water, and freedom from wild weather, there a farm would be found.

The men who sailed to Iceland from western Norway and the Norse colonies of the British Isles were Vikings. As such, they were daring and resolute, proud and self-reliant. A man's concept of honor was more important than his devotion to the gods. Life was to be lived vigorously and death was no cause for fear.

The sagas say these settlers left their ancestral estates to escape a king's harsh rule. Historians believe that the majority were land-hungry, fame-hungry men, and women like Aud the Deep-Minded, who came to Iceland to satisfy their strong ambitions. Whatever the reasons, Iceland was singularly fortunate in its founders. Courageous, aristocratic, and with a fertile cultural heritage, these people settled in small, scattered family groups. They raised sheep, cattle, and horses, hunted, fished, and traded.

The large landowners stayed on their estates, distributed land, exacted obedience, and dispensed justice. They were fiercely equal and independent. No king or earl lorded it in Iceland. Indeed the very core of the country was the landowning farmer. Unlike the more feudal societies to the south, women and children enjoyed both respect and legal rights. There were some slaves, usually foreign captives taken on trading and raiding expeditions, but they too could look forward to eventual freedom.

Despite the absence of an overlord, by the first quarter of the tenth century some men were definitely more equal than others—thirty-six to be exact. These men were great chieftains, descendants of the more aristocratic of the original four hundred settlers, such as Aud's twenty followers. They were able to dispense impartial justice to lesser men, but when there was a falling out among themselves, the strongest took the law into his own hands and dealt out his own kind of justice.

A central authority was needed to control the resulting disorders, and in the year 930, the thirty-six chieftains constituted themselves the Althing, or General Assembly. It met annually in the summer at Thingvellir under the presidency of the Law Speaker, who was elected by the chieftains. All freemen who owned land could vote in the Althing, but the real power rested exclusively with the chieftains. As you will see when you read *Hrafkel's Saga,* going to law was a risky business, doomed to failure without the support of one or more chieftains.

In spite of its imperfections, the annual meeting of the Althing in its impressive setting of mountains, chasms, lake, and plain was a national event that served as a unifying cultural force. Here, a whole nation gathered to hear the law proclaimed, to lodge their suits, to buy a sword, to sell land, to marry off a daughter, to display their skills. Indeed for two weeks of the brightest and longest summer days, Thingvellir was turned into the gay and busy capital of a unique country.

I first came across Iceland and its history while doing research on Leif the Lucky and his voyages to North America. That the Icelanders had been brave sailors and bold explorers came as no surprise, but nothing had prepared me for the reality of their literature.

The word "saga" brought to my mind fantastical stories of the gods and overly-heroic exploits of dragon-slaying adventurers. Instead, I came across the Icelandic Family Sagas—simple in style, realistic in detail, objective in tone, with a strong emphasis on characterization through dialogue and action. No heroes and gods here but real men, women, and children, and the events of their lives—births, battles, weddings, wars, friendships and games, travels and homecomings, feuds and lawsuits—in the Iceland of 930 to 1030.

Intrigued by what I read, I took time off from Leif the Lucky and set out to discover how and why a poor and remote island people produced a literature so uniquely interesting in style and scope.

Part of the answer can be found in the Scandinavian-Celtic heritage of the people themselves. Scandinavians of the Viking Age had excelled in the visual arts, as had the Irish. But in Iceland, nature itself set the limits upon the expression of this culture, for the volcanic stone was unsuited for carving, there was little timber and no natural source of metal. The creative force was channeled into words. By the end of the tenth century, Icelanders had supplanted native poets in the courts of Norway and Denmark. From that time through the fourteenth century, a powerful and varied literature flowed from Iceland: histories, poetry, sagas of the Scandinavian kings, lives of the saints, and the greatest contribution of Iceland to world literature— the prose narratives known as the Family Sagas.

Nature played a further role in fostering this vigorous creativity. No outside work could be done during the long dark days of winter, and thus there was plenty of time to write stories and plenty of people eager to pass the endless time in reading. Nature, by being stingy with winter fodder, had been generous in providing writing material. Since cattle couldn't be fed in winter, they had to be slaughtered. Vellum to write upon is made from calfskin. There still exist over seven hundred vellum manuscripts in Old Icelandic.

After the year 1000, when Christianity was voted the national religion of Iceland, acquaintance with sacred books and a growth in literacy further increased both reading and writing. Many of the anonymous authors of the Family Sagas were churchmen, but they wrote as educated laymen and not as servants of the Universal Church. They wrote of the heroic age of their country from the perspective of the strife-torn thirteenth century, and they created a literature that is the very soul of the Icelandic people.

A Note on Pronunciation

Hrafkel's Saga is written in Old Icelandic, and although it is not that different from the present day language, authorities differ on the rules of pronunciation. I have simplified some of the spelling for the sake of reading pleasure, and for the same purpose here are two simple guidelines to pronunciation: all syllables are stressed equally, and *j* is always pronounced as if it were *y*. The *H* in Hrafkel is virtually silent.

BARBARA SCHILLER
New York City
1972

1

HRAFKEL WAS fifteen when his father's ship sailed to the Eastfjords of Iceland and put in at Breiddale.

The serpent-prowed ship carried household goods, livestock, and retainers, for Hrafkel's father Hallfred would not live in a Norway ruled by a hard-handed king.

They were not alone. Hrafkel knew that more than a hundred chieftains like Hallfred had already settled in Iceland and that many more were even now gathering their retainers and readying their ships for the Iceland passage.

Hrafkel was a handsome boy with a fair skin and a straight nose. He had keen gray eyes and a fine head of curly auburn hair. He was vigorous and intelligent, an enterprising and promising youth.

Hallfred took his family and followers across the moor that lay north of Breiddale and built a house. He was a man who recognized good luck when it came his way. When in a dream a voice told him to move west across Lagarwater, Hallfred promptly did so, although it meant leaving a year and a half of hard work behind him. But within less time than that, Hallfred's livestock increased and so did the number of his followers.

It was Hrafkel's custom to explore the countryside when he was not working on his father's farm. Soon he knew the mountains and moors, the dales and the rivers better than any man in the Eastfjords.

One summer's day Hrafkel came to an uninhabited valley that stretched southward between two branches of the Jokuls River. The glacier was grim in the background, but the meadowlands were gay with flowers and lush with grass. It seemed to Hrafkel the finest farming land he had ever seen.

That evening he asked his parents for his inheritance, explaining that he wanted to start a farm of his own. His mother would have kept her only child at home a while longer, but she joined her husband in allowing their son to have his way.

Hrafkel built a house in the valley. It struck people as very large for a young man barely twenty. He called his home and farmstead Adalbol. Now a house, no matter how impressive, is an empty shell if it lacks wife and children, so Hrafkel married the flaxen-haired Odd-bjorg. She was good-looking and even-tempered and considered the best match in the Eastfjords.

When Hrafkel was well settled at Adalbol, he had a temple built and dedicated it to the god Frey. So much did Hrafkel love the god of fertility and growth that he had this temple made of wood brought from Norway. He filled it with objects of the choicest work-manship and sacrificed only the finest oxen before Frey's statue. Indeed, Hrafkel did more—he bestowed upon Frey a half-share of his choicest possessions, in-cluding the wind-swift stallion Freyfaxi.

Hrafkel laid claim to the entire valley and gave land only to those men who would accept him as their chieftain. As he grew rich and powerful, Hrafkel's self-confidence turned to arrogance, and his strong will led him to acts of ruthlessness. Anyone who disagreed with Hrafkel received neither justice or mercy. Those whom he considered his enemies were forced from their farms or killed. He put himself above the law and refused to pay compensation to the families of the men he killed.

His family, his household people, and his sup-porters loved him, for to them he was kind and con-siderate and just. As for the other men of the region, they knew only too well that Hrafkel was the most powerful of the chieftains in the Eastfjords.

2

ACROSS THE RIVER from Adalbol lived a man as different from Hrafkel as any man could be. Thorbjorn was
his name. In his youth Thorbjorn had been handsome
and strong, but he had grown old before his time. He
was of a distinguished family, and his farmstead had
once been a fine property. But Thorbjorn had bur-
dened his house with too many children and his land
with too little care, and so neither prospered.

One spring day Thorbjorn spoke to his eldest son
Einar. The boy was tall and able to do well anything
he put his hand to. Thorbjorn had been postponing this
talk for some time.

"Einar, the other children are getting big enough
to help me run the farm, so you will have to look else-

where for work. A boy of your ability will have no trouble. I love you more than my other children, but poverty and too many mouths to feed have driven me to this. The others will learn to be good workmen, but you are capable of doing much more with your life."

"Why didn't you tell me this earlier when hiring for the work year was just beginning?" Einar replied. "By now all the good jobs have been taken, and I don't much fancy working at what others have refused."

Thorbjorn had no answer to this and didn't look Einar's way as the boy walked off.

The next morning Einar bridled his horse and rode to Adalbol. Hrafkel had always been a good neighbor, and certainly he hired more men than anyone else. Hrafkel was sitting in his hall and gave Einar a pleasant greeting. The boy asked for work.

"Why have you come to me so late?" asked Hrafkel. "Of all the youths in Jokulsdale, you are the one I would have hired first. Now there is nothing left except a job beneath your worth."

Einar thought he knew what this job might be, but he asked Hrafkel to explain.

"It is almost time to move my livestock up to the summer pasturage, and I have not yet hired a shepherd."

Einar was prepared for this answer and replied that he didn't care what he did as long as he received full keep for a year's time.

"That you shall have in return for herding fifty milch ewes and gathering in the firewood for the dairy maids and the herdsmen at the pasturage.

"But," continued Hrafkel, "there is one condition. No one other than myself is allowed to ride the gray stallion, Freyfaxi. So much do I love him that I have sworn a great oath in Frey's temple to kill anyone who rides him. You will see Freyfaxi often, for he grazes with his mares in the upper valley. But remember that no matter how urgent the need, you must never ride this horse. To do so means death. The mares that run with my Freyfaxi are yours to ride as you please."

Einar swore that he would never ride the forbidden stallion, particularly since there were other horses to use if need be.

"Good," said Hrafkel. "You know the old saying —he who gives warning goes free of blame. Now return to your father's farm, collect your belongings, and come back to Adalbol with my warm welcome."

3

EINAR TOLD Thorbjorn his plans for the coming year, packed his clothes, and left with his father's blessings.

When summer came, it was time to drive the livestock to graze in the high pastures of the upper valley. Einar herded his ewes up to the highlands near the Grjotteigs River. A dairy was there and quarters for the dairymaids and herdsmen.

For all that his was a lowly job, Einar took pride in doing it easily and well. So able a shepherd was he that midsummer had come and gone without his losing a single sheep.

Then in a fog and a drizzle twenty sheep strayed from the flock. Einar searched every pasture for them, but without success. The other herdsmen counseled him to wait until the fog lifted, and impatient though he was, Einar knew this to be good advice.

He waited almost a week. Then early one morning Einar, standing at the door of his hut, saw the mist lifting to the south.

Now if he could only find the twenty ewes unharmed. As Einar thought of the missing sheep and the time already lost, he noticed the horses down by the river.

What better way to speed his search than to catch and ride one of Hrafkel's fine mares? Quickly Einar gathered up a bridle and saddle cloth and walked toward the herd.

The mares bolted. Einar was a notably swift runner and very good with horses, but now he chased them without success. Breathless, he stopped. The mist had completely lifted, and the morning was wearing on. The mares had galloped away. Only the stallion remained, as still as if he were rooted in the earth.

Einar looked at Freyfaxi. The stallion's pale coat and black mane glistened in the sunlight. Certainly there was good reason for this ride, and Hrafkel would never find out about it. For when it was over, Einar would rest the stallion, feed him by hand, and groom him until he gleamed.

Einar walked closer to Freyfaxi. The stallion tossed his head. Einar bridled Freyfaxi and fixed the saddlecloth on his back. He mounted the stallion and off they went.

Never had Einar known a horse like this. It was like riding the wind. Fast and far they rode, but when six in the evening came, Einar knew he must turn back and drive in the rest of his flock. So eastward they went toward the river. As they passed a ravine, Einar heard the bleating of sheep. There were his twenty missing ewes as sound as on the day they strayed away. He drove them in with the rest of the flock and headed home, well content.

Now it was time to tend to Freyfaxi. The stallion was panting with exhaustion, and every hair of his fine gray coat was wet and dripping. But no sooner did Einar dismount than Freyfaxi reared up, neighed loudly, and raced away.

Einar ran as he had never run before and almost laid hands on the bridle. But the stallion went wild, and Einar could not come that close again.

Down the valley Freyfaxi went at a great gallop, never stopping until he came to the main door of Adalbol.

Hrafkel was at table when he heard a neighing outside the hall.

"Surely that couldn't be Freyfaxi?" Hrafkel asked a serving man to go to the door.

The man returned with the news that it was indeed Freyfaxi, and in a sorry state, too.

Hrafkel went outside to see what had happened. At first he couldn't believe what his eyes told him. Then Freyfaxi pawed the ground impatiently, and Hrafkel's growing rage gave way to concern for the exhausted stallion.

"You've been ill-treated, my champion, and that grieves me. You did well to come to me, for I shall avenge you." Hrafkel stroked the horse's tangled mane. "A groom will tend to you, Freyfaxi. Then return to your herd. Tomorrow I shall see you again."

4

HRAFKEL SLEPT so soundly that when morning came his wife Oddbjorg was surprised to see him put on the dark blue clothes of death. She turned away as her husband mounted his horse, axe in hand, and rode up toward the highlands.

He arrived at milking time. The dairy women greeted him, and Hrafkel asked after Einar. They pointed to the sheepfold. There he was, lying atop the wall, counting his flock.

Hrafkel rode over and asked Einar how he was getting on.

"Not so well. Twenty ewes were missing for almost a week. However, they've all been found and are safely in the fold."

"I'm not worried about the sheep. Hasn't something more serious happened, Einar? Haven't you ridden Freyfaxi?"

Einar was standing now. He hesitated and then looked directly at Hrafkel. "I can't deny that I have done that."

"You own up to your guilt like a man, and that doesn't surprise me. But I cannot understand why you rode the only horse that was forbidden to you."

"I tried with all my might to catch one of the mares," explained Einar, "but they suddenly grew shy and bolted. Only Freyfaxi stood still."

Hrafkel dismounted. "I would forgive you a first offense if I had not sworn a solemn oath to Frey in his own temple. My faith tells me that nothing goes well for those who break an oath to Frey."

Einar's eyes spoke the terror his tongue could not. Hrafkel drew the axe from his belt. He killed Einar with a single blow.

As Hrafkel rode away, he saw Freyfaxi on the other side of the river. He waved to the stallion and then continued down to Adalbol. There Hrafkel told his news and sent a man up to the highlands to herd the sheep. He ordered this new shepherd to provide a decent burial for Einar.

But the people at the pasturage had been very fond of the boy, and when the new shepherd came he found they had already buried Einar on a hillside, and raised a cairn of stones over his grave.

5

WHEN THORBJORN heard of his son's death, his first
thought was to kill Hrafkel. But desperate as he was,
Thorbjorn soon realized the outcome of such an at-
tempt would most likely be his own death. There was
nothing to be gained by making his children orphans.

Thorbjorn fetched his horse and, with the tears
still wet on his face, rode over to Adalbol. He found
Hrafkel in the home meadow, near a storehouse. "You
have killed my son," said Thorbjorn, "and I'm here to
find out what you are going to do about it."

Hrafkel took the old man's arm and walked toward the manor house.

"You and I have been good neighbors for a long

time, Thorbjorn, so I can freely admit that Einar's death is the one killing I regret. If only the boy hadn't ridden Freyfaxi in spite of my warning."

Hrafkel paused and shook his head. Then he went on. "I shall now give you proof of how much worse I regard this killing than any of the others I've ever done.

"For as many years as you choose to live on your farm, I shall supply you with milk in summer and meat in winter. Whenever you decide to give up farming, you are to come here to my house and I shall look after you for the rest of your days. Furthermore, I shall see to it that your sons and daughters have the means to get a good start in life. And if there is anything you ever need, you must ask me and I shall see that it is yours."

Hrafkel waited for the old man to answer. Thorbjorn said nothing.

"I know," said Hrafkel, "that everyone will agree with me that this is generous compensation for your son's death."

Thorbjorn stopped before the door to Hrafkel's hall. "I will not accept your offer."

"What do you want then?" asked Hrafkel.

"I want us to settle this matter before the judges at the General Assembly."

Hrafkel looked surprised. "Do you plan to bring a lawsuit against me?"

Thorbjorn nodded.

Hrafkel smiled; it was a thin smile. "Then you consider yourself my equal. We can never be reconciled on such terms."

Thorbjorn untied his horse and left Adalbol. He rode straight down to his brother Bjarni's house.

Now as poor as Thorbjorn was, so Bjarni was rich. And whereas Thorbjorn had a houseful of young children, Bjarni had two grown sons. The elder, Sam, was a wealthy man, a skilled lawyer, and most conceited. He lived in the northern part of Jokulsdale. The younger brother, Eyvind, was a sea-going trader who had traveled all the way to Constantinople where he had lived for a time. Eyvind was noted for his wisdom and had received many favors from the Emperor of the Byzantines.

Thorbjorn found Bjarni seated in his hall and told him everything that had happened.

"I am here, Brother, to ask for your help in my lawsuit against Hrafkel."

To which Bjarni replied that rich though he was, he certainly didn't consider himself Hrafkel's equal.

"He has crushed men twice as powerful as me. No, Thorbjorn, a wise man knows his limits. You acted like a fool in refusing Hrafkel's offer, and I want nothing to do with this matter."

The brothers did not part on good terms. Thorbjorn had many harsh words to say about the quality of Bjarni's courage before he slammed the door of his brother's house behind him.

Now Thorbjorn rode northward to Leikskalar, his nephew Sam's house. A serving man answered the door, and when Thorbjorn asked for Sam, the man went to get him.

Sam had bright blue eyes and a round face and was quick-moving for a man of his size. He had always liked his uncle and gave him a warm welcome. But when Sam invited Thorbjorn to stay and received no answer, he realized something was wrong.

"What has happened, Uncle, that you are so heavy-hearted?"

Thorbjorn told him how Einar had been killed.

"It's hardly news that Hrafkel has killed someone. He uses his axe very freely."

"That may be," replied Thorbjorn, "but this time the blow struck one of your kinsmen."

"Did you try to get any compensation from Hrafkel?"

Thorbjorn told his nephew exactly what he had been offered.

Sam looked thoughtful. "I've never known Hrafkel to give so much as a penny's worth of compensation, and now he has made you a remarkably generous offer.

"Stay the night with me, Uncle, and in the morning we'll ride over to Adalbol. We will approach Hrafkel humbly and find out whether his offer still holds. If we handle this matter carefully, I am sure Hrafkel will behave generously."

"I am sure of no such thing," replied Thorbjorn. "Furthermore, Hrafkel's offer is no more to my liking now than it was when he made it. I've come to you because I want you to help me bring a lawsuit against him."

Sam did not show the impatience he felt at the old man's words. "That will be no easy thing to do, Uncle. In my opinion Hrafkel would be a very hard man to oppose in court."

Thorbjorn struck his fist against the door. "No wonder you young men never get anywhere! Either you make obstacles where none exist, or you turn your eyes away from your obligations and pretend they aren't there."

Sam tried to protest, but Thorbjorn kept on talking.

"I must be the only man in all of Iceland with such gutless relatives. You, Nephew, are quick enough to take on petty lawsuits, but in a matter this urgent you seem to have forgotten your reputation as a good lawyer. And when word gets around that you have refused me, I doubt if much will remain of that reputation."

The old man's face was red with anger, but his eyes were wet with tears.

"Uncle," said Sam, "how will you gain if I take

your case and we are both thoroughly humiliated at
the General Assembly?"

"It will be a great comfort to me if you take my
case, no matter what the outcome."

"I shall do it then, but only because we are kinsmen. And I want you to know that in helping you, I am
helping a fool."

With that, Sam held out his right hand and formally took over the case from his uncle Thorbjorn.

6

IT WOULD BE almost a year before the General Assembly met, so Sam did not have to hurry the preliminary proceedings.

First he saw to it that a group of neighbors were present at a nearby mountain farmhouse. Then he rode up to this place and before these witnesses gave formal notice of the charge against Hrafkel for the killing of Einar.

The people of Jokulsdale had much to gossip about that winter. Was Sam's courage equal to his conceit? What would happen if Hrafkel lost his temper?

Sam kept his own counsel, but he was well aware of what was being said. When winter had given way to spring and summons day came, he rode over to Adalbol and formally served a summons on Hrafkel for the killing of Einar.

There was no more talk about the probability that Sam's conceit was greater than his courage.

As for Hrafkel, he found the whole affair very amusing, although of little importance.

Now Sam rode through the valley and cited nine neighbors who would act as his witnesses when the General Assembly met in four weeks' time.

Not once did Sam display any nervousness or fear about what might happen to his case and himself at Hrafkel's hands.

As for Hrafkel, he behaved as he always did when it was time for the seventeen-day journey to the General Assembly. He sent men down into Jokulsdale to gather his followers. This year seventy well-armed men followed Hrafkel east and south to the lava plains at Thingvellir for the two-week session of the Assembly.

With Hrafkel gone from the district, Sam busied himself gathering followers. But aside from his nine neighbors, only vagrants agreed to follow him. Sam provided these men with food and clothes and weapons. With old Thorbjorn riding beside him, he led his force north and then south by a route that would get them to Thingvellir three days before Hrafkel.

When they arrived, Sam found a booth far from the place where the men of the Eastfjords usually stayed. He had it roofed over and well-furnished by the time Hrafkel and his seventy followers rode into Thing-vellir.

Hrafkel fitted out his booth among the people of the Eastfjords and set about entertaining and visiting those chieftains with whom he was on good terms. When he heard that Sam was at the General Assembly, he laughed as if it were the best of jokes.

This General Assembly was very well attended. Every chieftain of importance had come with his followers, and Sam felt confident that among so large a gathering he would certainly find a powerful chieftain whose influence, aid, and support would help his suit.

So off he went to call upon each chieftain in his booth. But no matter how shrewdly Sam worded his request, the answer was always the same. No one would risk his reputation in a quarrel with Hrafkel.

The chieftains reminded Sam that Hrafkel had always made sure by threat, force, and fear that no man ever got the better of him in a lawsuit.

Weary, Sam returned to his booth. He and Thorbjorn became increasingly dispirited and fearful that the only result of their lawsuit would be humiliation and dishonor. So great did their dismay grow that neither uncle nor nephew was able to eat or sleep.

EARLY ONE MORNING after a very restless night, Thorbjorn shook Sam's hammock.

"Wake up, Nephew. I can't sleep a bit, and I want to talk with you."

Sam, who had been thinking rather than sleeping, got himself up and dressed. "Let's go to the river and wash. Lack of sleep has dulled my wits. Perhaps cold water will sharpen them again."

The two men walked down to the Oxar River below the bridge.

"There," said Sam, "at last my head is clear. Now, Uncle, what did you want to say to me?"

The old man was sitting on the river bank staring

into the water. "It is my opinion that we should get ready to leave for home immediately. I tell you, Sam, it's obvious to me that humiliation is all that we shall ever find here."

"Now isn't that interesting!" answered Sam. "I seem to recall that I said the very same thing when you first came to me about this lawsuit. I also remember that you questioned my courage and my ability when I expressed doubts about the wisdom of suing Hrafkel."

Sam sat down next to Thorbjorn. "It is for these reasons that I will not give up until I know it is completely beyond hope to achieve anything here."

Thorbjorn covered his face with his hands and wept, so moved was he by Sam's words.

The lawyer looked away, and it was then that he noticed a man walking from a booth downriver and on the western bank.

Sam thought he knew every man of importance at the General Assembly; but here was a man of unusual distinction, and a stranger. He was tall, yet slight of build. His face was ruddy and handsome, and his fine head of chestnut hair had a light streak in it. He wore a tunic the color of a spring leaf, and his sword was of exceptionally fine workmanship.

Sam jumped to his feet, pulling Thorbjorn with him. "Stop your moping. We must cross the river and meet that man."

Thorbjorn had to move along quickly to keep up

with his nephew. As they approached the tall stranger, he greeted them and asked their names.

They told him, and Sam asked who he might be.

"I am Thorkel Thjostarson," said he. "A Westfjorder by birth and descent."

"And a chieftain?" asked Sam.

"Hardly that."

"A farmer then?" said Sam.

Thorkel said he was not and ventured no further information, although he appeared most pleasant.

Sam asked, "What manner of man are you then?"

"A footloose sort. I've been away from Iceland for seven years, seeing what there is to see and doing what I wanted to do. Much of that time I was in Constantinople where I was a liegeman of the Emperor. I've been home for over a year and staying at Thorskafjord with my brother Thorgeir."

"Is he a chieftain?"

"Indeed he is," replied Thorkel. "His authority is recognized throughout Thorskafjord and in many other parts of the Westfjords as well. Thorgeir is outstandingly skillful with arms, and there is no sport at which anyone can best him. He is powerful of build and handsome of face. A leader of men in every respect."

"Is he here at the Assembly?"

"Yes, with seventy of his followers."

"Would you like to give us some help?" Sam asked.

"You're forthright enough, aren't you?" said Thorkel. "What do you need?"

"A powerful chieftain to help us," said Sam. "We are bringing suit against Hrafkel of Adalbol for the killing of Thorbjorn's son Einar. I am a lawyer, and we can rely on my pleading as long as we have the benefit of your support."

Thorkel looked at old Thorbjorn and then at Sam. "But I am not a chieftain. I have already told you that."

"Why should a man such as you have been disinherited?" asked Sam. "Surely you are as much a chieftain's son as your brother Thorgeir?"

"I never said that I was deprived of my share of the chieftaincy. Before setting out on my travels, I entrusted my authority to Thorgeir, and when I returned, I saw no need to take it back. As I have said, Thorgeir does everything well. He is highly-principled, brave, and always eager to add to his reputation. He is just the sort of man to give you the support you need."

Sam looked glum. "Without your help we will get nothing from him."

"I shall be on your side," said Thorkel, "for I like your spirit, and your cause promises some excitement. But more than that, to avenge a kinsman's death is a necessary and honorable thing to do. It is a just action worthy of any man's help.

"Now," he continued, pointing to the booth from

which he had come, "go into my brother's booth. Everyone there is still asleep. You will find two hammocks near the inner gable that belong to me and my brother. He has had an extremely painful boil on his foot ever since we came here and has hardly slept at all. But last night the boil burst, and Thorgeir has been asleep since. To ease his foot, he has rested it on the footboard of his hammock."

Thorkel turned to Thorbjorn. "You go in first, old man. When you reach Thorgeir's hammock, stumble and grab the footboard. Be sure to catch hold of his bandaged toe."

Sam frowned. "I am sure you mean to be helpful, but this doesn't seem like a good plan to me."

Thorkel replied, "If you don't want my advice, then go to someone else for help."

"Come, Thorbjorn," said Sam. "Let's go to Thorgeir's booth."

8

THORBJORN WAS beginning to tremble with nervousness as he and Sam entered the chieftain's booth.

The old man didn't have to pretend to stumble. His poor eyesight and nervousness made him unsteady and clumsy.

Sam held back as his uncle stumbled and fell against Thorgeir's hammock. There was an angry shout when Thorbjorn wrenched the chieftain's throbbing foot.

Then Thorgeir threw off the bedclothes and sat bolt upright. "Who is crashing around here like a blinded bull? Haven't you any respect for the sick?"

Sam and Thorbjorn couldn't think of a thing to say.

It was well that Thorkel walked into the booth then.

"Come, come, Brother," he said, "there's no need to get so angry about this, for you'll come to no harm. A man's actions are often worse than his intentions, and never more so than when he has a heavy weight on his mind. You are suffering from the pain in your foot, a pain that only you can feel. This old man is suffering because of the death of his son. That is a pain only he can feel. He has no means of redress, and no one to help him. Surely it is understandable that he is pre-occupied?"

Thorgeir was standing now and putting some weight on his foot. "Since I didn't kill his son, I don't see why he should take it out on me."

"He wasn't," Thorkel explained. "Thorbjorn came at you harder than he intended because his eyesight is poor and his legs unsteady. Actually, he came to you hoping that you would help him with his lawsuit. And, Thorgeir, wouldn't that be a fine deed?"

Thorkel didn't wait for an answer. "Thorbjorn's cause is just and honorable, for it is duty, not greed, that compels him to take action over the death of his son. Not a single chieftain will help Thorbjorn and Sam, so timid a group of men are they."

"Whom are they accusing?" asked Thorgeir.

"Hrafkel of Adalbol killed Thorbjorn's son for no reason," replied Thorkel.

"This is certainly not the first time Hrafkel has done that," said Thorgeir. "I feel exactly as the other chieftains do. I have no obligation to help and no desire to get involved with Hrafkel. Any man foolish enough to sue Hrafkel receives only failure and humiliation for his pains. Hrafkel sees to that, which is why no one will meddle with him unless forced to by great necessity."

"Perhaps," Thorkel said, "if I were a chieftain I would feel that way too. But the way things are now I feel that the best adversary for me is the man who has never been beaten. In my opinion any chieftain who attempts to restrain Hrafkel will gain great credit. And if he fails as the others have, there is no cause for humiliation."

"I see now," said Thorgeir, "that you are determined to help these men. If I hand over the full authority of our chieftaincy to you, you will be in charge and can do whatever you want. Exercise the authority for as long as I have, then afterwards we can share the chieftaincy between us. What do you think of this plan?"

"I think," Thorkel replied, "that in making plans for my future I would do well to go where my words carry more weight than they do here."

"Brother, you are offended." Thorgeir said. "I cannot have any differences stand between us, so I will help these men whatever may come of it."

Thorgeir turned to Sam and Thorbjorn. "What do

you two feel yourselves capable of contributing to the success of your suit?"

"As I said earlier, we need the backing of a powerful chieftain," Sam replied. "But since I am a lawyer, I will conduct the actual pleading myself."

Thorgeir was considerably relieved. "That makes it easier to help you. Perhaps we will succeed in cutting Hrafkel down to size. Certainly the men who can do that will win honor for themselves. Now go back to your booth, prepare your case, and be cheerful, for you must show a great deal of confidence if you are going to face Hrafkel in court. However, do not tell anyone of our promise to help. Hrafkel must continue to feel that your lawsuit is of no account."

By the time Sam and Thorbjorn returned to their booth, they were in the best of spirits. Their followers were surprised and encouraged by this sudden change of mood.

9

WHEN THE COURT convened, Sam called on his men to
march with him up to the Law Mount. He noticed immediately that Hrafkel was not among the chieftains
present.

Before the assembled court Sam named his witnesses and called upon them "to testify that I give notice
of an action against Hrafkel Hallfredson, inasmuch as
he assaulted Einar Thorbjornson and inflicted upon
him a grievous wound, which did cause Einar's death."

Sam went on in a ringing voice to present his case
in a manner that was both forthright and in complete
accord with the law of the land.

While he was talking, Thorkel and Thorgeir with
a strong force of men came close up to the Law Mount.

Every farmer from the Westfjords stood with them, and it was apparent to all at the court that the two brothers did not lack friends.

Sam then named witnesses "to testify that I call upon Hrafkel Hallfredson or whomever shall take over the defense on his behalf to hear my oath and my charges and all the evidence I shall plead against him."

There was loud applause, but no one came forward to speak on Hrafkel's behalf.

Instead, some men pushed their way through the crowd and ran to Hrafkel's booth.

When he heard what was happening on the Law Mount, Hrafkel acted at once. He summoned his army of followers and gave them their orders.

"We'll march on the court and break it up by force. Little men like Sam must learn that it is a risky thing to bring suit against me."

Hrafkel and his followers set off in strong procession, but they never got to the Law Mount. So great was the throng of people pressed one against the other around and up the slopes of the Mount that Hrafkel was kept away from court by sheer force of numbers. He couldn't hear what his prosecutor was saying, much less present his own defense.

Sam concluded his case by demanding "that Hrafkel Hallfredson be sentenced to full outlawry on this charge. And as an outlaw, he shall not be fed nor forwarded nor helped nor harbored."

Now it became apparent that there were powerful

men who wanted to see Hrafkel humbled, for then and there the judges declared him an outlaw.

Such surprising news spread quickly through the crowd and reached Hrafkel as he stood thwarted in the noisy throng.

Back he went to his booth, shoving aside anyone in his path. He had his horses brought around immediately and led his silent men away from the lava plains of Thingvellir.

Hrafkel rode east across Lyngdale Moor and from there east to Sida. He didn't stop until he reached Adalbol. But once home, Hrafkel's dark mood left him, and he behaved as if nothing unusual had happened.

Sam and Thorbjorn were in no hurry to leave the General Assembly. Many people had good reason to be happy about Hrafkel's humiliation, and Sam and his uncle swaggered about enjoying their praise.

A few days before the Assembly was to be dissolved, Sam thanked Thorkel and Thorgeir once again for their help.

"So you are pleased with the outcome of your lawsuit," Thorgeir said.

Sam replied that such indeed were his feelings and that everything was going very well for him and Thorbjorn, too.

"Do you really think you're that much better off than before?" Thorgeir asked.

"Yes," said Sam. "Hrafkel has suffered a much-needed humiliation, and that's all to the good."

"It's one thing to be awarded a decision, quite another to enforce it," Thorgeir said. "Hrafkel is not a full outlaw until the court of confiscation has been held."

Sam nodded. "Yes. I must be leaving here to capture Hrafkel, and I don't have much time. The court of confiscation has to be held at Adalbol within fourteen days after the General Assembly has been dissolved."

"You know your law," replied Thorgeir, "but if I know people, Hrafkel is at his home and planning to remain there. In my opinion he will keep his chieftaincy no matter what you try to do. If you are lucky enough, you might be able to stay on your farm and talk about Hrafkel the Outlaw. But you will forever be at Hrafkel's mercy, such as it is."

"That doesn't frighten me at all," said Sam.

"Then I'll be the first to say you're a brave man."

Thorkel spoke now. "Sam, we would not desert you at this time. Having gone this far with you, we feel it is our duty to help until you have settled your affairs with Hrafkel and can live in peace. We will go back to the Eastfjords with you. Do you know a road that is not much traveled?"

Sam said they should follow the same route that he had taken to Thingvellir. He was so pleased now that he felt as if he could go that distance at a run.

10

THORGEIR PICKED forty of his best men and saw to it that Sam's forty followers were as well armed and well mounted as his own men.

They followed Sam's route, and although they didn't tire their fine horses, neither did they spare them. At sunrise on the very day the court of confiscation had to take place, Sam led his force across the Jokuls River.

As the last of the men rode over the bridge, Thorgeir turned to Sam. "Now that we are in your home country, tell us the best way to take Hrafkel by surprise."

"That's simple. Follow me."

Sam turned abruptly from the path. He urged his horse up a mountainside and then along a ridge. When they reached the mountain above Adalbol, Sam dismounted. He turned to Thorgeir and Thorkel. "Let's all dismount and leave our horses here. Twenty men can stay behind to watch them. The rest of us will descend on Adalbol. The slope is very steep here, and we'll move much faster without horses."

The men set off at a run. They raced headlong down the slope, dashed across the meadow, and reached the manor house a little before rising time. None of the people were up yet. Sam ordered the men to ram the door with a log and charge inside.

Hrafkel was seized and dragged from his bed. Struggling, he was forced outside along with the other able-bodied men of his household. Oddbjorg and her sons were driven into a room with the old men, women, and children.

Outside in the meadow there was a long, high beam for drying clothes. It extended from the back of the main house to a storehouse. Thorkel ordered Hrafkel and his men led to this place.

Hrafkel had stopped struggling. He looked at Sam and then at Thorgeir and Thorkel. "Spare the lives of my men. They have done you no harm, and it will bring you no credit to kill them. I am not going to beg for my life. You can kill me without any discredit to yourselves. I only ask that you do not torture me, for there is nothing to be gained by that."

Sam did not reply. He told his men to tie Hrafkel's

arms behind his back. "Do the same for the others, and then see if there is any more rope in the storehouse."

They found a quantity of stout rope strung on pegs.

At Sam's orders, Hrafkel and his men were hung from the clothes beam by their ankles.

"You are getting what you deserve, Hrafkel," said Sam. "I don't suppose you ever thought the day would come when you would be humiliated as you are now."

"Sam," said Thorgeir, "you are wasting time."

He turned to his brother. "To hold the court of confiscation, Sam must find a rocky mound within arrow-shot of the house, but away from furrowed fields and meadows. The court can only be held with the sun due south, so we must hurry. Will you go with Sam?"

"No," said Thorkel. "I will stay here with Hrafkel."

So Thorgeir and Sam went off to hold the court of confiscation. It took them some time to find a suitable place and go through the formal proceedings. When they returned, Thorkel had ordered Hrafkel and his men cut down and laid upon the ground. Their eyes were all bloodshot, and they did not move.

Sam stood beside Hrafkel and looked down at him. "I'm offering you a choice of two things. Death immediately or life on my terms. If you choose life, you must leave Adalbol with all of your people and the few belongings I shall allot to you. Your lands and your chief-

taincy will become mine. Furthermore, neither you nor any of your descendants are ever to settle again on this side of Fljotsdale Moor. What do you say to that?"

Hrafkel replied, speaking slowly. "Many men would prefer a quick death to such a disgrace. But I shall choose life. Not only do I have many people dependent on me, but I have two young sons. I do not like to think what might happen to them if I should die now."

Hrafkel's bonds were cut loose, and he got to his feet. It took him some time to do this. He shook hands with Sam as a token of agreement. Then after his men were freed, he helped them to stand. Sam watched this with his hands on his hips.

Later that day Hrafkel departed from Adalbol taking with him all his people. He carried a spear, the only weapon Sam allowed him. Hrafkel looked back just once. He saw Freyfaxi in the distance, standing still among his herd.

Thorkel said to Sam, "I don't like what has happened. To have spared Hrafkel was a deed you'll regret a lifetime."

"I can understand," said Thorgeir, "that you would want to stretch out Hrafkel's humiliation. But if that was your plan you shouldn't have tortured him. By treating him that way, you have guaranteed that he will seek vengeance. That is my opinion."

Sam replied, "It isn't mine."

"All right," said Thorkel. "But remember that the price you must pay for satisfying this whim is eternal vigilance."

"That's a price I am more than willing to pay," Sam answered, turning away.

Sam's wife joined him at Adalbol, and they set up housekeeping in fine style. He established Thorbjorn at his old farm at Leikskalar, telling his uncle to use the farm as if it were his own.

Then Sam gave a magnificent feast for all those men who had been Hrafkel's supporters. He offered to be their new chieftain, and they accepted him.

The day after the feast Thorgeir and Thorkel came to Sam with some advice. They told him to be kind and considerate, an open-hearted and generous chieftain always ready to help his supporters.

"Then only the worthless among them will not stand fast to you when you are in need," said Thorkel.

"We have given you this advice," Thorgeir said, "because you are a brave man and we want you to succeed in all things. But the most important advice is what Thorkel has already told you. Keep your eyes open, stay on guard, and don't ever forget the old saying—it's warm work watching out for the wicked."

Before they left, the brothers asked that Freyfaxi and his herd be brought in so they could inspect these famous horses.

"I think the mares would be useful for farm

work," said Thorgeir. "But the stallion doesn't seem unusual except in the trouble he has caused. Since Frey owns him now, let's return this horse to his master."

The gray stallion was led to the high cliffs by the river where Hrafkel had built his temple to Frey. There the horse was killed, and the temple plundered and burned to ashes.

When Thorkel and Thorgeir were ready to leave, they exchanged vows of everlasting friendship with Sam. He gave them gifts of the most splendid sort, and they parted on the warmest terms.

11

WHEN HRAFKEL left Adalbol, he traveled eastward until he came to Lagarwater. There, at the head of the lake he found a farm for sale. Although the price was little enough, Hrafkel had to purchase it on credit since he needed to buy tools and provisions for his people.

The land was extensive, but the farm was sadly lacking in buildings, which was why it was sold cheaply.

There was a lot of talk in the Eastfjords about Hrafkel and his new farmstead. "It's a good thing to see the haughty humbled," some said. "Yes, him on a beggarly farm and the other living fine like an earl at Adalbol," said others.

Sam enjoyed this talk, but Hrafkel had no time to listen to such gossip. He worked his people hard, and himself hardest of all, to raise a stately farmhouse and sturdy outbuildings before winter set in.

There was no temple at the new farm, for when Hrafkel heard that Freyfaxi had been killed and Frey's temple burned, he said, "It is folly to believe in the gods, for each man makes his own luck for good or bad." From that time Hrafkel never set foot in a temple to make sacrifices or worship again.

The first year at Hrafkelstead was one of severe hardship. There was a great deal of work, no comforts, and very little food because Hrafkel would allow no slaughtering. He kept every kid and calf right through the winter. So carefully did he tend his animals that only a few failed to survive.

His livestock proved very productive. They gave almost double the normal yield of young. When summer came Hrafkel and his people were able to forget the hunger of winter, for never had Lagarwater teemed with trout as it did then.

Hrafkel continued to work hard and manage well. Within a few years he became a very rich and powerful chieftain. It was not long before everyone in the district was eager to sit or stand just as Hrafkel wished.

There was still land east of Lagarwater, but Hrafkel would allow no man to settle there until he had promised him his support. In return for this, Hrafkel pledged his protection. Hrafkel's chieftaincy increased until his authority extended over many more miles and men than had his former chieftaincy in Jokulsdale.

Hrafkel was a different man now. Hardship had cut down his arrogance but sharpened his abilities. He had learned to be more reasonable and calmer in all things. Before, people had feared him, but now he was well liked by everyone.

Sam had prospered, too. He added more luxuries to his household and, being fond of show, filled his hall with admiring guests. He was very popular with his supporters, for he never forgot the brothers' advice to be kind and quick to help.

Sam and Hrafkel met every year at the General Assembly, but they never spoke of the past. Sam often remarked to his friends how Hrafkel had changed and now seemed quite content to lead a quiet life on his estate. But except for these meetings, Sam gave Hrafkel little or no thought.

And so it was that six years passed in this peaceful fashion.

12

ONE SUMMER'S DAY a ship put in at Reydafjord. It had crossed the open seas heavily laden, and its captain was Eyvind, Sam's brother. Eyvind had always been handsome and strong. Now, after seven years abroad, he had also become a man of great wealth and noble bearing. He was gentle and patient, a man of integrity who remembered the past and understood the present. Eyvind had hardly made land before he was told about Sam and Hrafkel's affairs. Eyvind, as was his custom, listened carefully.

When Sam heard of Eyvind's arrival, he immediately had his horse brought around and rode eastward over the moors to Reydafjord. The reunion of the two was an occasion of the greatest joy and affection; for not only did Sam love Eyvind as a brother, but he regarded him as an adviser who could solve any problem. Sam invited Eyvind to come to Adalbol and spend the winter there. Eyvind gladly accepted and said, "First would you ride home and send pack horses for my baggage?"

While Sam did that, Eyvind had his ship hauled ashore and made ready for the winter. When Eyvind had seen to his cargo, he loaded the sixteen pack horses and set out for Adalbol.

There were six men in the party: two were Sam's servants, three were sailors, and the sixth was Eyvind's serving lad, a young Icelander who was a distant kinsman. Eyvind had rescued this boy from the worst poverty, taken him abroad, and looked after him like a brother. This was a fine deed, and everyone agreed that few men were Eyvind's equal.

Eyvind and his companions crossed Thordale Moor and rode over the ridge into Fljotsdale. They wore gaily-colored clothing and carried bright shields. At mid-morning they rode around the head of Lagarwater and forded the Jokuls River.

An old woman, a servant at Hrafkelstead, was washing clothes down by the lake. When she saw the men passing by, she looked hard at them. Then she bundled up her wash and ran to the farm. Throwing the bundle down near the woodpile, she scurried inside the house. Hrafkel had not gotten up yet, his sons were in the hall, and all the farmhands were out in the fields, for it was the haying season.

The old woman started to cluck away. "It's true. The saying is true. The older a man gets, the feebler his courage. A man's courage grows so weak that he can't even avenge his own honor, or so it seems to me. Still, I must say it does seem strange in a man who was once thought brave."

Hrafkel was up now. He wondered what the old woman was gabbling about.

She talked on. "But do you know what seems even stranger to me? That a man who as a boy was nothing much goes abroad and comes back the very model of manhood, more so indeed than many a chieftain I could name."

Hrafkel was standing by the old woman now. He listened closely.

"Eyvind Bjarnason has returned. He has crossed the Jokuls River with six men. He's dressed fine as a flower and is riding toward Adalbol carrying a shield that sparkles in the sun. A fit target for revenge that one."

Hrafkel cut her short. "You're a spry one, old woman. Go south to the farm of Sigvat and Snorri. Tell them to come to me with their best men as quickly as possible."

He sent another servant to the farm of Thord and

Halli. Both pairs of brothers were outstandingly brave and able men.

Hrafkel turned to his sons. "If luck is with us today, Sam will be mine to do with as I find proper. I have watched him grow overly secure and complacent in his high position. I knew it would only be a matter of time before he took a wrong step and gave me the chance for revenge. But with Eyvind to advise him, Sam will never make any mistakes. As the old woman said, Eyvind is a fit target for revenge. Get your weapons."

Hrafkel had his best farmhands called in from the fields. Now there were eighteen men well-armed and well-mounted. Accompanied by his sons, Hrafkel and his party rode swiftly across the river as the other men had done before them. Hrafkel wore dark blue clothes and carried an axe.

By this time Eyvind and his companions had reached Fljotsdale Moor and were crossing a swampy area where the mud oozed up above their horses' knees. West of this bog the ground was a stony wasteland. As they were picking their way along, the servant boy happened to glance back.

"Eyvind," he said, "we are being followed. Eighteen or twenty men are riding after us. Their leader is a tall man dressed in the dark blue clothes of death. Although I haven't seen him in a long time, I think it is Hrafkel."

"What does it matter?" Eyvind asked. "We have

nothing to fear from him. I've never done Hrafkel any harm. He's probably riding west to meet some friends."

The boy shook his head. "I have the feeling it's you he wants to meet."

"I'm not aware that there has been any trouble between Sam and Hrafkel since they made their agreement," said Eyvind.

"Nevertheless," replied the boy, "I think it would be best if you rode ahead to Adalbol. You'll be safe and so shall we since Hrafkel is not the sort to seek vengeance against a man's followers."

"I don't even know for sure if it is Hrafkel," said Eyvind. "What a laughing stock I would be if I took to my heels without further proof."

They had crossed the stony ground now and were riding through another bog. Their heavily-laden pack horses slowed them down considerably, and they had just cleared the bog when their pursuers rode into it.

"It is Hrafkel," said the boy. "Ride fast, Eyvind, and you'll soon be at Adalbol. Hrafkel and his men will not be able to make good time through the bog. Ride fast, I beg you."

The other men in the party also urged Eyvind to seek safety.

"I am not going to run away from a man I have never wronged," replied Eyvind.

He led his companions westward up across one ridge and then over another. When they reached the slope of the second ridge, he saw a turf knoll whose sides were eroded by the wind. There Eyvind dismounted and told his companions to hobble their horses and let them graze for a while.

"We shall soon know upon what errand these men are riding," Eyvind said.

With that, he and his companions climbed to the top of the knoll and gathered stones for weapons.

When Hrafkel and his followers came to this place they turned from the path and rode toward the knoll. Hrafkel said not one word to Eyvind, but attacked instantly. Eyvind defended himself skillfully and with great courage.

The servant boy, judging himself not strong enough to fight, untied his horse and galloped over the ridge and down to Adalbol. When Sam heard what was happening, he sent immediately for his nearest neighbors.

Twenty well-equipped men rode with Sam to the scene of the assault. They arrived at the knoll just as Hrafkel was galloping away.

Eyvind lay on his back in the trampled grass. "Oh, my brother, have they killed you?" cried Sam. His hands shook as he looked for some sign of life in his brother, but Hrafkel had done his job well. Eyvind and all his men were dead. Twelve of Hrafkel's men were dead too, but six, including his sons, were even now riding east with him toward Hrafkelstead.

"We'll go after them," Sam said, and there was desperation in his voice. "Their horses are tired, and ours are fresh. We might just catch them before they can ride down from the moor."

Pursuers and pursued rode hard that day. But when Sam reached the edge of the moor and saw Hrafkel a long way down the slope, he called off the chase.

"Hrafkel will easily reach his own place and gather all the men he needs. We must turn back now or fall into his hands."

So Sam turned back with no gains for his efforts. When he came to the place where Eyvind lay dead, he set to work and raised high a burial mound over Eyvind and his companions. This place has been known ever since as Eyvind's Hill.

Sam told his men to round up the pack horses and drive them down to Adalbol.

He rode home immediately thereafter and sent word to all his supporters to come to Adalbol at sunrise "for a trip eastward across the moor."

13

WHEN HRAFKEL reached home that evening, he told his news, ate his dinner, and gathered up a force of seventy men.

No one knew Fljotsdale Moor better than Hrafkel. He led his men at a good pace until they came, completely unexpected, to Adalbol.

Sam was surprised in his bed, seized, and led outside to Hrafkel, who waited near a storehouse.

"I don't suppose," said Hrafkel, "that you ever thought the day would come when you would be humiliated as you are now. But it has come about that your life is in my hands, and I shall be no less generous than you once were to me. I'm offering you a choice of two things, Sam. Death immediately or life on my terms."

"I prefer to live," Sam replied, "although I suspect that one alternative will be quite as harsh as the other."

Hrafkel nodded. "You can be sure of that. But remember, Sam, if you had behaved better in the past, then so would I now."

Sam said nothing.

Hrafkel continued, "You are to leave Adalbol with all the goods that Eyvind brought with him, but nothing else. You are to go back to Leikskalar and live there on your farm. I shall resume my chieftaincy in this district and take back my estate and possessions, which I see you have increased vastly. You shall receive no compensation for Eyvind's death or that of his companions. I don't think that what was done to them was any worse than your torturing me and my men as revenge for Einar's death. You made me a refugee from the law in my own district, but I shall allow you to live in peace in your own home. Go to Leikskalar, behave as befits your station, and there will be no trouble between us. Forget your place, and things will indeed go ill for you."

Sam accepted the terms with no comment and moved down to Leikskalar with his family. Old Thorbjorn was dead now, but some of his children were still at Leikskalar. Sam let his kinsmen stay on, but he had little to do with them or anyone else that winter.

As soon as the days grew longer, Sam had three horses shod. One was for him, one for his servant, and the third for their baggage. Thorskafjord was Sam's destination, and Thorkel and Thorgeir gave him a warm welcome when he arrived.

Sam spent a week at Thorskafjord enjoying the rest. Thorkel had just returned from four years abroad and had many good stories to tell. When the time seemed right, Sam told the brothers what had happened between himself and Hrafkel and asked for their help and support once again.

Thorkel replied, "When we left the Eastfjords six years ago, we had done everything possible to guarantee your success in keeping what you had won."

Sam nodded his head in agreement.

Thorgeir spoke up. "I am not surprised that this has happened. We urged you to kill Hrafkel. Had you had the good sense to listen to us—or the compassion to have spared him and his men torture—things would have been very different today."

Sam looked away from Thorgeir as Thorkel spoke again.

"You won much, but Hrafkel won more, for he learned from his experience and you did not. In spite of our warning, you even forgot the past and came to look upon Hrafkel as a man not worth fearing. Hrafkel has shown himself to be by far the better man. He left you in peace and waited in patience for the opportunity to avenge himself. No, Sam, we do not see any wisdom in burdening ourselves further with your poor judgment and bad luck."

Sam listened to all of this in silence.

"But," said Thorgeir, "we have not forgotten our vows of friendship. Bring your family here and live under our protection, for surely that will be more pleasant than living alongside Hrafkel."

When both brothers were finished speaking, Sam replied that he would like his horses made ready for the journey home. His voice was as even as he could make it.

Thorkel and Thorgeir wanted to give Sam fine gifts, but he refused these, too. "All that I want is your help and support. To refuse that and offer gifts instead shows a mean spirit on your part."

Sam made no further effort to control his anger. He and the brothers did not part on good terms.

As Sam rode back to Leikskalar, he knew only too well that the rest of his days would be lived in Hrafkel's long shadow.

As for Hrafkel, he stayed at Adalbol and enjoyed not only great prestige and honor, but the respect of his neighbors as well. He did not live to be an old man, and he died in his bed with his family around him.

So ends the saga of Hrafkel.